Stories to Grow By

Patty Saves the Day!

A Tale in Which Patty Discovers Her True Gift

by Kathryn Wheeler
illustrated by Darcy Bell-Myers

In Celebration®, Grand Rapids, MI

Library of Congress Cataloging-in-Publication Data

Wheeler, Kathryn, 1954-
   Patty saves the day! : a tale in which Patty discovers her true gift / by Kathryn Wheeler
; illustrated by Darcy Bell-Myers.
      p. cm. -- (Stories to grow by)
   Summary: Although she hopes to impress the other prairie dogs with her singing, Patty
discovers that she already has an important special talent. Includes a Bible verse and
facts about prairie dogs.
   ISBN 0-7424-0012-3 (hardcover)
   [1. Prairie dogs--Fiction. 2. Self-acceptance--Fiction. 3. Christian life--Fiction.] I.
Myers, Darcy, ill. II. Title. III. Series.

PZ7.W5655 Pat 2000
[E]--dc21
                                                                    00-024705

Credits

Author: Kathryn Wheeler
Cover and Inside Illustrations: Darcy Bell-Myers
Creative Director: Annette Hollister-Papp
Project Director/Editor: Alyson Kieda
Editor: Sara Bierling
Cover Design: Ruth Ostrowski-DeKorne
Page Design: Darcy Bell-Myers

ISBN: 0-7424-0012-3
Patty Saves the Day!
Copyright © 2000 by In Celebration®
a division of Instructional Fair Group, Inc.
a Tribune Education Company
3195 Wilson Drive NW
Grand Rapids, Michigan 49544

For information regarding permission write to:
In Celebration®, P.O. Box 1650, Grand Rapids, MI 49501.

Printed in Singapore

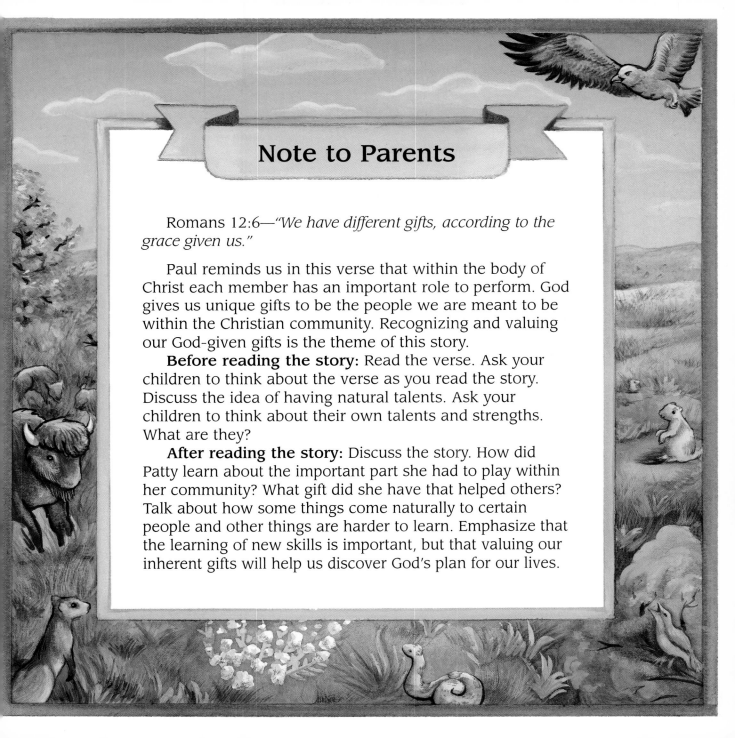

Note to Parents

Romans 12:6—*"We have different gifts, according to the grace given us."*

Paul reminds us in this verse that within the body of Christ each member has an important role to perform. God gives us unique gifts to be the people we are meant to be within the Christian community. Recognizing and valuing our God-given gifts is the theme of this story.

Before reading the story: Read the verse. Ask your children to think about the verse as you read the story. Discuss the idea of having natural talents. Ask your children to think about their own talents and strengths. What are they?

After reading the story: Discuss the story. How did Patty learn about the important part she had to play within her community? What gift did she have that helped others? Talk about how some things come naturally to certain people and other things are harder to learn. Emphasize that the learning of new skills is important, but that valuing our inherent gifts will help us discover God's plan for our lives.

Patty Prairie Dog had been taking singing lessons for weeks, but she still felt nervous. She cleared her throat. Molly Meadowlark nodded in encouragement. They were at the north end of Prairie Dog Town, which stretched out from the vast, rolling plain to foothills covered with scrub pine.

"Ready?" asked Molly. "Try not to throw your arms up in the air this time."

"Ready," Patty said. She closed her eyes and heard again the beautiful, flutelike tune that Molly had just sung. She would sing it, too; she *would*. Patty took a deep breath and opened her mouth to sing like a bird.

5

"Yip, yip, YIPPITY YIP!!" sang Patty, her arms thrown high in the air. She opened her eyes and looked at Molly.

"Hmm," said Molly. "I actually think that was a little better."

"Really?" asked Patty, overjoyed. "Should I do it again?"

"Hmm," said Molly again. "I think that's enough for now. Time to go home and practice." As Patty headed back toward the town, Molly called out, "Practice a *lot*, Patty!"

Patty hurried
toward the backdoor
tunnels at the edge of
town. As she drew nearer, sentries
threw their arms into the air, stretched
up on their tiptoes, and started yipping a
pattern of yips that meant, "No cause for
alarm, everybody. It's only Patty. She's in a
hurry, and she's wearing her new gingham dress today."

7

Patty sighed.
Keeping her singing
lessons a secret had been hard in this busy
town where everyone knew everyone else's
business. She dove into a tunnel. She
tiptoed past the nursery where her
mother was busy with the five new
babies, hurried down the long passage to her
room, and plunked down on her soft bed.
"I'll sing at the Harvest Festival. I will amaze everyone!"
Patty promised herself. Then she cleared her throat and
began singing scales very softly. "Do, re, mi, yip, yip, YIP!!!"

8

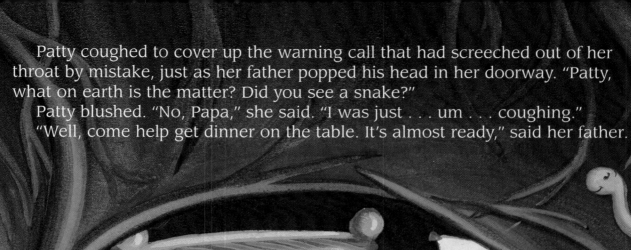

Patty coughed to cover up the warning call that had screeched out of her throat by mistake, just as her father popped his head in her doorway. "Patty, what on earth is the matter? Did you see a snake?"

Patty blushed. "No, Papa," she said. "I was just . . . um . . . coughing."

"Well, come help get dinner on the table. It's almost ready," said her father.

9

The next day, Patty rushed out to the pine trees and waited for Molly to soar across the long, bending grass. Patty waved at a fawn-colored speck on the horizon. As Molly swooped down to the pine tree, she said, "You have great vision, Patty! I don't know another prairie dog who could have seen me from that distance."

Patty blushed at the compliment. Keen eyesight was the best thing a prairie dog could have. Patty knew that her only protection against a fox or a hawk was to see it before it saw her.

Molly said, "Try that song from yesterday."

Patty stood up and closed her eyes. In her mind, she saw the whole town seated around long tables at the Harvest Festival dinner. She stood in front of them in her best dress. She opened her mouth wide and began to warble like a lark: "Trill, trill, yip, yippity, YIP!"

Patty opened her eyes. "I think I lost the tune for a minute," she said.

Molly sighed. "I think you *did have* the tune for a minute, though." After listening to dozens of attempts, the little meadowlark advised, "Just keep practicing . . . and keep your fingers crossed."

When Patty hurried home that day, she was so late that her mother was standing in one of the doorways waiting for her. "Patty, we were worried sick about you!" said her mother as they hurried back down the tunnel together. "Where were you?"

Patty knew she could no longer keep her secret. In the living room, she turned to face her mother, her father, and the babies. "I have a surprise. I am going to sing at the Harvest Festival!" she announced.

"Sing?" echoed her father. "Prairie dogs can't sing."

"Yes, they can!" Patty insisted. "I know *I* can. Even Molly Meadowlark thinks I'm good enough to keep practicing!"

The news of Patty's performance swept like a grass fire through the town. Questions peppered the air: "What are you going to sing, Patty? What are you going to wear? How long have you been singing?" Patty practiced for hours each day. Finally, during Patty's last lesson, Molly said, "Well, I can't honestly say that you sound *exactly* like a meadowlark, Patty. But you don't sound like any prairie dog I've ever heard."

Patty was thrilled. She knew she would be a great success.

On the day of the festival, Patty paced nervously up and down the town square. Patty's mother proudly set out five carrying baskets. Each held a baby dressed in white with a ruffled bonnet. The other prairie dogs cooed at the babies as they carried grasshopper stew, short-grass salad, grass-root soda, and other treats to the tables.

Amid the buzz of activity, Aunt Prudence Prairie Dog pushed her way up to the nervous Patty and said, "Singing? Hogwash! Prairie dogs were not made to sing." Patty held her tongue. "Where's your mother? Did she make sneezeweed soufflé again this year?" Patty nodded. "I have to make sure I get some of that," declared Aunt Prudence and hurried off.

"Hogwash," Patty whispered, her paws clenched. "I'll show her!"

14

Finally, the great moment arrived. Hundreds of prairie dogs took their seats as Mayor Pete Prairie Dog led Patty up to the podium. "Before we begin our harvest meal, here's the treat we have all been waiting for. Miss Patty Prairie Dog will now SING!"

Patty forced herself to gaze up into the sky to avoid staring at the sea of expectant faces. And as she looked, she saw a tiny brown speck zigzag toward the town. Patty's eyes widened. She threw her arms up into the air.

"Yip, yip, YIPPITY YIP, HAWK!" she screamed.

For a brief moment the prairie dogs froze, and then they burst into action. Mama Prairie Dog tossed basket after basket into the nearest tunnel, each baby basket sliding neatly down the curved tunnel and landing in the living room. One of Patty's sisters grabbed a tablecloth as her mother whisked her away. Dishes flew up into the air like white birds. Aunt Prudence tripped and ended up with a drippy yellow beret of sneezeweed soufflé on her head. Patty dove into an escape route underneath the podium. By the time the hawk arrived, he found nothing but overturned tables and scattered chairs.

Patty was miserable. "I failed," she whispered as she trudged down a long tunnel that led to her house. She found her family gathered in the living room.

Patty's father hugged her. "Patty, you were marvelous!" he said.

"No, I wasn't," Patty mumbled. "I didn't get to show everyone that I can sing."

"But that's all right, Patty," said her mother. "You already have a great gift. You have the best eyesight of any of us, and today your gift saved a whole town of prairie dogs."

17

Patty's father hugged her again. "You should be as grateful for your true gifts as we are, Patty."

Patty smiled. She looked around the room and said, "I'd be grateful for some sneezeweed soufflé. Didn't you bake an extra one, Mama?"

"Yes, I did," Mama answered, "because last year your Aunt Prudence ate a whole one all by herself."

Patty grinned. "I think she ended up with a whole one this year, too."

As they sat down to eat, Patty gave thanks for her family and their safety and for the knowledge that she was already special, just as she was.

A Note About Prairie Dogs

Prairie dogs live in highly organized communities in prairie grasslands, with hundreds of animals living in one town that can stretch for miles. Their tunnels and burrows are part of their defense system against enemies. Built so each prairie dog can dive to safety easily, burrows for family groups can have as many as 70 tunnel doorways.

These intelligent animals have excellent memories and use different patterns of calls to describe different predators and even humans. Scientists have found that once a human has visited a prairie dog town, the animals will remember that person for years and will give the same call to announce his or her presence. When making a warning call, a prairie dog will throw its arms up into the air and throw its head back. The call sounds something like the bark of a small dog.

Prairie dogs stand about ten inches (25 cm) high and weigh from one to three pounds (0.5 to 1.4 kg). They eat grasses along with some insects and wildflowers. Members of the same family will embrace and sniff each other in a posture that resembles hugging and kissing. Young prairie dogs have been seen playing tag, King of the Hill, and tug-of-war, using the same "rules" as human children.